D0007885

DISCARDED

| DATE DUE | | | |
|---|---|---|---|
| | | | |
| | | | |
| | | | |
| | | | |
| | | | |
| | | | |
| | | | |
| | | | |
| | | | |
| | | | |
| | | | |
| | | | |

J.J
GIL
   Gill, Janie Spaht.
   Balloons

PORT JERVIS FREE LIBRARY
138 Pike Street
Port Jervis, NY 12771

# BALLOONS

© copyright 1998 by ARO Publishing.
All rights reserved, including the right of reproduction in whole or
in part in any form. Designed and produced by ARO Publishing.
Printed in the U.S.A. P.O. Box 193 Provo, Utah 84603

ISBN 0-89868-342-4–Library Bound
ISBN 0-89868-404-8–Soft Bound
ISBN 0-89868-343-2–Trade

# A PREDICTABLE WORD BOOK

# BALLOONS

Story by Janie Spaht Gill, Ph.D.
Illustrations by Elizabeth Lambson

*Sept. 02 Forest House 13.10*

ARO PUBLISHING

PORT JERVIS FREE LIBRARY
138 Pike Street
Port Jervis, NY 12771

4

# The pink balloon became a hog.

# The green balloon became a frog.

8

# The yellow balloon became a duck.

9

10

# The red balloon became a truck.

12

The orange balloon became
a hat.

14

# The white balloon became a cat.

16

# The purple balloon became a mouse.

17

18

# The blue balloon became his house.

20

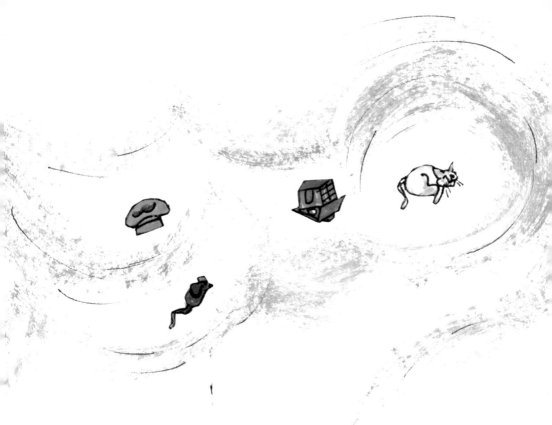

# Then wind blew that day,

and all my balloons sailed
away.